LIFE BEFORE DAMAGED
VOLUME 7

THE FERRO FAMILY

BY:

H.M. WARD

www.SexyAwesomeBooks.com

COPYRIGHT

This book is a work of fiction. Names, characters, places, and incidents are either the product of the author's imagination or are used fictitiously, and any resemblance to actual persons, living or dead, events, or locales is entirely coincidental.

Copyright © 2015 by H.M. Ward
All rights reserved.

No part of this book may be reproduced, scanned, or distributed in any printed or electronic form.

LAREE BAILEY PRESS
First Edition: July 2015
ISBN: 9781630350789

LIFE BEFORE DAMAGED

Volume 7

MAY I QUOTE YOU ON THAT?

August 22nd, 9:05pm

"No."

Pete's sapphire eyes snap to mine. He's been avoiding my gaze ever since he stopped kissing me, but now I have his full attention. He takes his hands out of his pockets and tucks them under his armpits, arms crossed tightly.

"What do you mean, no? Moving isn't optional; my mother doesn't want you disappearing on her again. Pack your bags and be ready in an hour. We have a nice guest suite waiting for you in my wing."

His normal arrogance is enveloping him like armor. It's what keeps him sane, but it shuts everyone out and costs him everything. I wonder if he knows. I wonder if he realizes what this barricade he erects around himself costs him.

Pete glances around Erin's loft, his handsome face curling into an unattractive sneer. It's obvious he thinks this is a hellhole. Where I see freedom and independence, he sees crumbling bricks and exposed pipes that are ready to collapse.

"Camp is over, Gina," he snaps at me. "You've been in the wild long enough. You don't need to slum it anymore, doing dishes or whatever it is you do around here."

Every muscle in my body becomes rigid, and my jaw locks tight. I feel my gaze narrow as I try to keep my hands off his neck.

"You prick! Are you that blind? Can you seriously look around and not see what I see?"

Pete's proud smile waivers for a second, but when he turns that blue gaze my way again, I see nothing but an arrogant man unable to see past his own nipples.

"Fuck it, Ferro." I throw up my hands and step toward him, head swaying as I walk. I poke his chest with my finger, one poke for each word. "I. Am. Not. Going. Anywhere."

Pete looks down at my finger on his chest. I leave it there for half a second. His chest doesn't rise and fall—he stops breathing—frozen in place. It's awesome for the three seconds it lasts.

Pete grabs my finger and pulls my hand into his, offering a panty-dropping look as he does it.

"We both already know what you really want."

Snatching my hand back, I jerk away from him. My face crumples as I spew whatever venom I can create.

"Bend over and suck yourself, Ferro. I'm not leaving. You can't make me and, if you try, I'll shove Erin's bat so far up your ass you'll have two dicks."

His jaw drops. Suddenly he blinks and steps back. His shoulders hunch forward a little, and he lifts his hands. I can't tell if he's afraid or laughing at me.

"This isn't funny! Stop being such an asshole for five minutes and think about someone else for once. My pre-wedding living conditions were never part of the deal. I signed on the line to pretend I have feelings for you in public places, to swoonily get engaged to you on New Years' Eve, and marry you in the summer. I'm doing those things. Nothing's changed, except one tiny thing that doesn't matter to you at all."

Pete's face softens. He steps toward me, tilting his head to the side inquisitively. His voice is soft when he speaks.

"What changed?"

I don't answer. He swallows hard, and the air fills with crushing silence. I grind my teeth in an attempt to shut up, but it doesn't work. That look on his face is wrong. It's like I just offered him a puppy. What the hell is wrong with him?

"Pete!" I yell his name and throw up my hands, exasperated. "Can't you see? I'm happy here! It's the first time in a long time that I'm laughing again. I smiled today. Do you know how rare that is? Especially after the person I love most sold me off like fricken cattle."

Pete presses his lips together. He takes a step toward me and places his warm hands on my arms. They're folded across my chest tightly, putting a barricade between us. His dark lashes lower as he studies my fingers.

"Gina—"

"Get lost, Ferro, or I'll hand her the bat." Erin's voice is dark and dangerous. I have no idea how long she's been standing there.

Pete ignores her and continues to watch me. He squeezes my arm. "Come with me. You don't have to prove anything."

Disgusted, my jaw drops and I step away from him. Pete's hands fall to his sides.

"I have nothing to prove to you. I'm enjoying caring for myself and pitching in around the apartment. My favorite thing, Master Ferro," I arch my eyebrow and smirk at him, "has nothing to do with sex or money. And I'm not giving it up yet, so go be a good little messenger boy and tell your mother I am staying right here. If she needs to contact me, she can call my cell phone."

Erin rips a piece of paper in half and hands it to me. I pull one of the pens from my hair. After jotting down my number, I stuff the paper in his hand.

"Now she knows where to reach me. If she's still not happy, she can stuff her opinions up her ass. Who knows? Maybe she'll like it and smile for a change."

Erin's eyes go wide. She mouths, DAMN, before disappearing into the bathroom. I know she's trying to give us space. She can't tell if I want him here or not. I can't blame her since I can't decide. One second he's great and the next he's an asshat.

Pete pushes his hair out of his eyes and smiles at the wrinkled paper. He smooths the note, folds it, and puts it in his pocket. His mouth quirks up to one side as a challenging expression transforms his face.

"Just one question?"

I glare at him. "What?"

"May I quote you on that?" He smiles and lowers his gaze before looking back up to meet mine. I think he's laughing inside. "I'm sure my mother would love to receive that message verbatim."

I stand there, tapping my one bunny slippered foot against the floor, arms folded over my chest.

My brows rise defiantly, implying I'm all backbone and not made of jelly.

"Go ahead. Use air quotes. Write it on her forehead if you have to, but get my point across: I'm not leaving."

Pete smiles that charming fake grin of his, and nods. He collects his helmet and heads toward the door.

"This is between you and her," he says over his shoulder. "I can't wait to see how it goes down. By the way, I love your outfit. I want you wearing that on our wedding night, friend."

Pete leans in and chucks my chin. I shake it off and frown at him. He looks me up and down, taking in my less-than-sexy pajamas. He places a hand on his chest, mocking a heart attack.

"Seriously, what guy wouldn't want his bride dressed like that?" With his sexy smirk in place, he winks at me. My stomach dips and falls into my slippers. Pete turns away before I can say anything and disappears through the door. Before it closes behind him, my bunny slipper flies across the room and hits the back of the door. I can hear him chuckling down the hallway as he disappears into the night.

HOUSEWARMING PARTY
August 25th , 9:45pm

Mrs. Ferro has been silent, which freaked me out at first. I half expected her to show up later that night.

Over the three days since Pete left with my message, the only repercussion of our conversation has been for a Ferro Family chauffeur to arrive for my convenience. He seems constantly available, shuttling me from place to place in a discreet black sedan, quiet and professional from the driver's seat.

While it appears to be a kind and generous gesture on her part, I know it's her way to ensure I don't make a mad dash for Syrupland and a new

Mountie boyfriend. I love Canada. Monitoring my movement is her way of intimidating me, but I won't give in. Constance Ferro will not dictate where or how I live—at least not until I marry her son. Until then, I intend to enjoy my life as best I can.

After dancing the weekend away at the swing club, Erin, Ricky and I close the festivities with a Sunday evening party at Ricky's place.

Ricky's loft is located directly below ours and could be a carbon copy, minus the paint stains and scattered artwork. Instead, his place has a retro, male bachelor pad look to it. Vinyl records, a vintage pinball machine, a pool table, and a collection of Betty Page posters in various stages of undress make the place feel vibrant and hip.

An earlier makeover shopping session with Erin was hellish in the moment, but so totally worth it in the end. With my new tight-fitting jeans, a plaid shirt tied at my waist, and Erin's masterful hair and makeup job, I resemble a 40's pinup model. Plus, the new threads look great with the leather jacket Pete gave me. Badass bonus!

Gina: 1.

Pete: no jacket.

I'm laughing again. A smile constantly lines my lips. My confidence is at an all-time high, and the party is in full swing, fun and upbeat, with people smiling, dancing and singing along with a karaoke machine up on the mezzanine. The brave and vocally blessed walk upstairs to perform while we dance like fans at a rock concert on the floor below.

Everyone here is a stranger, save Erin and Ricky, but a group of particularly boisterous men catch my attention. They seem to own this party. They are definitely thrill seekers, with an adventurous beach-boy, skater thing going on. Whenever a member of their group is done singing on the mezz, they let themselves fall, arms folded across their chests, from the top floor into the waiting arms of their friends below. I screeched so loudly when the first guy fell, the whole room noticed and laughed. It was classic Gina. Erin will never let me live it down. And my face was red enough that even in the shadows, people could tell.

Old Gina would have hidden under a table for the rest of the night. New Gina owns it. I threw up my arms and spun around, laughing. It didn't make my blush go away, but everyone cheered. If you got it, own it. I'm embracing my inner dork, and she's thriving.

Erin and I dance among the crowd of people. It feels so great to let go and forget life for a while. I close my eyes and let the rhythm take over. My arms and hips do as they want, and I become one with the music. It's liberating.

Dancing has always been my salvation and my escape. This is where I excel. When I'm dancing, I can be the person I want. I'm music's slave, losing myself in a trance of beats and lyrical sensuality.

The room warms as people pack in tighter. My clothes stick to my slick skin as I work up a sweat, not caring how I look. My red lips spread across my face in a wide, happy smile. The music shifts suddenly and we adjust.

The new song is a bit edgier, with a dirty, gritty rock beat to it. I pause to find the beat, and then surrender to the music once more. I'm in my own world, grinding my hips against an imaginary dance partner, hands above my head.

Suddenly, the hair on the back of my neck stands on end as I feel a pair of eyes on me. I glance up and, among the crowd of people dancing, dark brown eyes stare into mine. It's one of the thrill-seekers. He's handsome, with tan skin and chestnut hair that has obviously passed the needs-a-haircut stage. It curls out at the ends and around his face.

He has the friendliest smile—it's warm—like butter. I love butter. I want to marry butter! I laugh and keep dancing.

I noticed Hot Guy earlier. He arrived a bit later than the others. They all greeted him with boisterous cheers and slaps on the back. Women have been flocking to him non-stop all evening, but he's staring right at me, smiling. It's not an icky, predatory look, either.

We both keep dancing on opposite ends of the floor, giving each other occasional glances and flirty smiles. Why would the hottest guy here be interested in me? My thoughts are interrupted by a familiar voice at the microphone.

"This one is for my bestie," Erin strangles the mic and continues, "and I need you guys to get her up here. Knowing her, she'll run out of the room crying within the next second. Gina, baby! Get your skinny, bony ass up here!"

Erin points a finger at me from the mezzanine and crooks it in a 'come here' way. Her evil smirk is on. The crowd around me follows her gaze to me, then shoves me toward the stairs of the mezzanine. I pass Hot Guy on my way up, and he puts a hand on my lower back, nudging me toward the stairs.

"Have fun, Mystery Girl," he whispers in my ear.

I turn my head around just enough to see him out of the corner of my eyes and say, "You may want to cover your ears, Mystery Guy. I've broken mirrors by singing in the shower."

As he starts to laugh at my comment, I run up the stairs to meet Erin. She hands me the second mic.

"I can't believe you made it up here without being carried," she yell-whispers. "I'm impressed."

Feeling bold, I grab the mic and talk into it while pointing my finger at the people watching me.

"Prepare to have your asses rocked off." They laugh. That sort of came out wrong.

Erin presses a button on the karaoke machine. The title of the song appears on the screen as the opening notes ring out from the speaker below. It's a popular song about surviving a bad breakup and coming out stronger, female empowerment in musical form. The crowd below cheers as they recognize the song. Hot Guy is looking up at me.

When the words start to flash across the screen, Erin and I give it all we've got. The vocal range of the song is much too high for me. I sound like a cat caught in an accordion. Screech, shrill. Screech, shrill. Wow, I suck. But I keep on signing, missing every single note. It's a spectacular failure.

As expected, some people cover their ears and cringe, but I don't run away. With Erin by my side, we lovingly massacre the song with our singing voices. I glance down at Hot Guy once in a while, and he just laughs, giving me a thumbs up.

We're bringing suckage to new levels. Someone is holding up their phone. You Tube, here we come. Instastar! I walk up to the edge of the stage and sing my heart out to the crowd, and they cheer on my fansuckingtastic rendition of the song.

Our performance eventually ends and everyone applauds and cheers our overwhelming mediocrity. Erin gives me a hug after which I hand her the mic and back up to the edge of the stage. Erin's eyes go wide.

"Gina, what the hell are you doing?"

I raise my eyebrows at her and look down briefly over my shoulder, making sure there are people below and that they have seen me. Hot Guy nods and moves in closer below the mezz. My heart pounds furiously, and I feel like I can fly. I'm invincible.

I can do this.

"Gina, are you fucking insane? Get back here!" Erin's face is a jumbled mixture of skepticism and terror. She doesn't think I've got the guts to do it, but she's also scared shitless that I might do it anyway.

I wave my fingers at her, smirking as I cross my arms over my chest and pivot. I clutch my shoulders, lean back, and let myself drop.

HELLO, MY NAME IS GINA AND I'M AN ADRENALINE JUNKIE
August 25th , 10:33pm

It feels like time is suspended. All sounds cease to register, except for the rush of air in my ears. Everything else—the music, the people cheering, Erin screaming my name—become a vague hum in the background.

My stomach stays up on that stage while my body plummets toward the floor.

"Holy fuck!"

I have no clue if anyone is going to catch me or not. The feeling is both frightening and exciting. It could end in two ways, one ends with cheering and me springing off the floor like a sprite. The other option will make me a permanent grease stain on Ricky's floor.

My descent ends suddenly, in a soft thump. Several faces are looking down at me, all smiling, some cheering. They caught me.

Thank God! It feels like my heart stopped beating for a while and only just started again. The rush is exhilarating, and I let out a laughing scream of joy. The guys that catch me put me down on my feet and give me congratulatory pats on the shoulder. I feel my face shift into a huge smile.

Up on the mezzanine, where I was just moments ago, Erin is kneeling at the edge, her hands holding on so tight that her knuckles are white, mouth gaping. What the hell did I just do?

"Very impressive, Mystery Girl. That took guts."

I turn around to see Hot Guy standing there, hands in his pockets and grinning at me. I can't help but grin back.

"Which part? The singing or the drop?"

"Both," he says, laughing and shaking his head, "but in very different ways. I've never heard a tone-deaf duet before."

I take a small bow, giggling. Someone grabs hold of my arm tightly from behind and swings me around abruptly.

"Gina! You scared the shit out of me! Don't ever do that to me again!" Erin has completely lost it. She's bouncing between scolding me and making introductions at the same time. Her hands fly all over the place like a Muppet gone wild. "Hey, Phil, good to see ya. Gina, this is Phil. Phil, this is Gina. Gina, what the fuck were you thinking?"

She's so beside herself it's funny, and I begin to laugh. "I'm fine!"

"Stop laughing, bitch! I need a smoke. You and I are not done discussing this. Don't do that to me EVER again, you hear me?" She waves a finger in my face as I try to stop giggling, but I still have a hell of a rush.

Erin stomps away and crawls out the window, onto the fire escape.

Hot Guy, I mean Phil, glances at me and then back at the window where Erin disappeared. "Wow. You really pissed Erin off."

"Yeah, she can be a little overprotective sometimes. So, it's Phil, right?"

I extend my hand and he takes it, but instead of giving it an introductory shake, he gallantly brings my hand to his lips for a kiss. The gesture seems familiar yet so out of place in this setting.

"And you're Gina. It's nice to meet you." Phil looks toward the dance floor and nudges his head. "Want to dance?"

"Actually, I'd prefer to sit down. My legs are shaking like I've got squirrels for bones." I laugh nervously. "Is that normal?"

Is that a normal question? No! What the hell, Gina? Who says things like that? As I mentally chastise myself, Phil takes my hand.

"Yeah, it's part of the adrenaline rush." He puts his hand on my lower back and escorts me to a nearby couch. He grabs two bottles of beer from the ice bucket on our way and hands me one. "You look like you need one of these."

"Thanks. Getting rid of squirrelly-legs is hard, but someone has to do it."

Phil has a funny expression on his face. Oh, fuck it. I screwed this meeting up. Now there's no way I can take this hot man home and make him my mistress. Mister? That can't be right. I take the bottle, uncap it, and take a swig. "What do you call a male mistress?"

Phil nearly chokes with laughter.

"I don't know. A man? Are you considering getting one and not sure what to Google?"

I have my beer in my mouth and laugh so hard I spew. I start choking and he pats my back while Ricky shrieks at me from across the room.

"Stop spitting beer all over my vintage rug!" He runs off to get paper towels.

"So, how do you know Erin?" Phil sits sideways facing me, one hand on the backrest, the other nursing his beer. "I've been out of town for the past few months, but this is the first time I've seen you here." He looks me up and down and grins. "And, believe me, if you'd been here, I would have noticed you." His eyes sparkle flirtatiously, appreciative and full of flattery.

If he knows Erin, he probably knows her past, that she came from money. I don't want to give my social status away. I don't want to make him uncomfortable or have him start acting fake around me just because my family is rich. I'm sick of the phonies like Anthony. That wound is still too fresh, and I don't care to repeat it.

"As of last week, I'm her new roommate. That's why you haven't seen me here before." That's all I offer. It's true, yet doesn't give anything away.

"I see. Well, from her reaction, I'd bet stage diving isn't your usual scene?"

"Hardly, but it felt great. Thanks for catching me. I like to eat pancakes but have no interest in being one." I smile at him as Ricky returns to spot clean the carpet.

"You keep your fluids to yourself! No stains on my couch either!"

Horrified, my jaw drops.

"What do you think we're going to do?"

"I don't know," he says throwing a roll of paper towels at me, "just clean it up when you're done!

That couch can't be replaced either! It's vintage 1940's velvet!"

"Yeah, from your Grandma's apartment," Erin yells from across the room. "Stop being a douche, Rick-rock, and come dance with me!" Ricky narrows his gaze on Erin. He excuses himself and a moment later, we hear her screech and giggle.

"So, did you like it?" Phil catches my eye again. "The diving part?"

I lean my head back on the backrest of the couch, looking up at the ceiling.

"That was so—awesome. It was a rush, fast and slow, crazy and sane all at the same time. I felt like I was falling through music with the way the bass is pounding. I'd do it again if I didn't think Erin would kill me afterward." I tilt my head to the side to look back at Phil. My cheeks are cramping up from the constant smiling. I want to feel this alive forever. Phil hums and taps his beer bottle with his finger.

"Have you ever tried skydiving before?"

My eyes go wide. Can this guy get any hotter? I sit up straight on the couch.

"Do you skydive?"

"Yep. So do a bunch of these guys." He gestures his beer bottle toward the room then takes a sip. "If you want to try it out, I can hook you up with a good instructor at the Drop Zone. Like, literally hook you up with him; would you be interested in a tandem freefall?"

Oh. My. God. I remember the rush I felt riding on the back of Pete's bike, the same way I feel in a toss while swing dancing, and the same way I felt falling off the mezzanine. I wonder what jumping out of a plane would feel like, free falling from so high up.

"I'm very interested."

'Hello, my name is Gina and I'm an adrenaline junkie.'

GET THE HELL OFF MY RUG!
August 25th, 11:27pm

Phil and I spend the next long while talking about skydiving and then move to stuff people usually talk about when they first meet: work, school, hobbies, travels. Phil is friendly, and our conversation flows easily.

"So the moment my masters in political science was done, I decided to backpack across Europe before starting my doctorate. I only just got back a couple days ago." Sitting back in my seat, I can feel the tip of his thumb brush up against my shoulder, moving back and forth, and it sends shivers everywhere.

There's no denying the little jolt of excitement his touch ignites within me. He's hot, smart, and everyone here wants his attention. People are either staring at us or interrupting our conversation for a quick acknowledgment from Phil. Women are asking him to dance only for him to decline politely.

How did I end up with the hot guy at the party sitting next to and talking to me? When did I become that girl? Nobody has ever flirted with Regina Granz before, yet Phil is flirting with me and it feels oddly wonderful.

I'm contractually obligated to Pete, but it's not a romantic relationship by any means. It's a business merger that will keep us out of jail. I'm not doing anything wrong; besides, we're not officially engaged yet. Pete's making the most of his last bachelor days, so why can't I?

This morning's newspaper featured a huge article on Pete's philandering ways. It featured a huge picture of Pete, surrounded by a group of drop-dead gorgeous women. The article read:

NOW INTERVIEWING FOR POSITION OF MRS. PETE FERRO

Pete Ferro, heir to the multi-billion dollar Ferro family fortune, was spotted Friday night crashing a sorority party in New York City. After treating all the young women to unlimited champagne, a select few were chosen to attend a private party in Ferro's private jet.

"It was like a fantasy," said NYU senior economics major Melanie Piper, of Washtenaw, Ohio. "Money was practically flowing from the onboard champagne fountain."

Sources close to the Ferro family speculate Ferro is currently under pressure to find a spouse. Others speculate he is just sowing his wild oats...

I couldn't finish reading the article. My fingers kept drifting across the picture, over his face, his eyes, and his lips. His mouth was smiling, but his eyes looked detached, devoid of emotion, like an empty shell.

Seeing him with those girls made me want to tear the page out, rip it to shreds, and scream profanities, but, at the same time, something inside me ached for him.

In this set of pictures, he looked miserable.

"Am I boring you that much?" Phil's hand squeezes my shoulder lightly, calling my attention back to our conversation.

"Sorry, no. Not at all. I guess I'm just coming down from the rush."

I shake thoughts of Pete out of my head. He's not going to ruin the next couple of months for me. Tonight has been perfect, and I won't let myself feel guilty for it. I have the attention of an attractive man who's not belittling me or pushing me away for someone better.

"Well," Phil stretches and slides his arm off the back of the couch, "I should get going anyway. I'm still on European time. If I don't get some sleep now, I'm going to crash in the car on the way home."

The disappointment takes me by surprise. My hot guy is leaving, and I want him to stay with me a bit longer. If I were Erin, I'd invite him up to my place for the night, but that's not me.

Phil pushes himself off the couch and holds out his hand to me. I take it, and he helps me up. He takes a step closer.

"It was really nice meeting you, Gina. Mind if I call you sometime? Maybe make good on my skydiving offer?"

My stomach does a few somersaults just being so close to him. One step closer and our bodies will be touching. A fluttering feeling blossoms inside me and I take his hand, lacing our fingers together.

This feels normal. Guy meets girl, guy and girl engage in friendly small talk, guy asks girl for her phone number, guy offers to push girl out of an aircraft in mid-flight.

Someone dancing behind me bumps into me roughly, and I go crashing into Phil with an unattractive oomph! He places both his hands on my hips to steady me and keeps me there, close to him. During the crash, my hands shoot up to hold onto his arms.

We both look at each other and laugh uncomfortably. Phil seems to feel just as awkward as me. He stares down at me, his fingers tighten over my hips as his gaze drops to my lips, and he finally breaks the silence.

"Gina? I want to kiss you right now, but I feel that I should ask you first. You have this untouchable vibe about you. Is that weird?"

Should I do this? My life isn't normal, and, even though this feels right, and this feels normal, I know it's not something within my reach.

Pete's free to do what he wants when he wants, and I've been aching for that kind of freedom, even if temporary. Lots of people have casual relationships that don't go anywhere, right? If two people feel a connection, it's not wrong to indulge a little, as long as no one gets hurt. No promises are being made, and none will be broken.

A kiss means something to me, but I don't want to live with regrets of wasted opportunities. I promised myself I'd make every moment count. Besides, this could be my last chance at feeling close to someone. Once married to Pete, I'll be off the flirting market for good. I'm not going to be the cheating wife, even when I know he'll cheat on me. I'll have no mister mistress.

I hold his arms tighter and rise on my toes, tilting my head slightly to the side as I bring my lips closer to his. Phil smiles and dips his head down slowly to kiss me.

It's a soft kiss at first, very sweet. Phil brushes his lips against mine, and it feels nice. He lets go of my hips and cups my face with his hands and presses in a bit more firmly. The fluttering intensifies with the kiss and my arms glide up along his arms and wrap around his neck.

Music and the sound of people laughing and singing surround us. I'm taken by surprise when I feel his tongue stroke my lips, and I hesitate. Before I make a decision to let the kiss deepen, I feel a slap on my back and hear Ricky's voice.

"Glad to see you two getting along. Now, get the hell off my rug."

The kiss breaks and I back up abruptly, my face flaming.

Ricky looks at us with a smirk. Have I mentioned that I hate PDA? Being caught kissing Phil sends my anxiety level soaring, and I need to get out of here.

I wipe my hand across my mouth as if the imprint of his kiss is glowing. Phil looks annoyed at Ricky for having interrupted us, but Ricky just keeps smirking proudly, snapping his suspenders against his chest and rocking on his heels.

I look at Ricky and murmur, "Asshat."

"Don't make me stuff paper towels down your shirt. As it is, you're busting the seams open."

I look down and realize that the knot is the only thing holding my retro shirt together. My lacy black bra is peeking out between lots of cleavage.

Score for cleavage!

Boo for showing everyone at once!

I don't adjust my outfit. Instead, I blink and act like I'm normally half dressed and kissing random hot guys. Jenny rides again!

"So, it's been great," I say backing up, "but I have to go. Ricky, great party, thanks. Keep that roll of paper towels to stuff your pants."

"Bitch," he says, laughing.

I don't pause. "Phil, it was nice meeting you. You can get my number from Erin. If you want to, you know, call me or whatever. But you don't have to do it. If you don't want to. I mean, if you have someone else that you might want to do, do that. With her. Or don't." I laugh nervously and twist my hands

together. I told him to do someone and call me.
"Yeah, that about sums it up."

Ricky barely contains his laughter.

Phil is smiling like I'm cute. He extends a hand in
my direction and opens his mouth to speak, but I
bolt from the loft, closing the door behind me.
Behind the closed door, I hear Ricky explode with
giggles.

I lean against the wall in the hallway and smile.
Despite the last few moments of complete and total
mortification, the evening was incredible. My phone
buzzes from my back pocket. I pull it out and look
at the screen.

Of course I want to call you, Gina. -Phil

I close my eyes and press the phone to my chest
while the fingers of my other hand brush up against
my lips, remembering the kiss we just shared.

FRIENDS
August 25th , 11:52pm

Back in reality, I stand just outside Ricky's door for a while staring at my girls, wondering what it would be like if they seemed this huge all the time. Looking at the shirt I make a mental note—check the button situation on vintage clothing before diving off a stage. Every single one popped. No wonder why all the guys were grinning at me. I synch up my knot to cover my bra, but now my midriff is showing, a lot.

I hear rapid footfalls echo through the cold, empty hall. The footsteps slow down and stop.

"Gina? Is that you?"

His voice startles me. Not because I was expecting to be alone, but because I wasn't expecting it to be him. Pete's voice has a way of jolting my heart like a defibrillator.

When I open my eyes, I see the glory that is Pete Ferro. Except the normal smirk is missing, the typical spark illuminating those blue eyes is gone, and his shoulders slump like he's carrying a mountain on his back. The cut on his cheek is healing, but there's still a faint line. No new bruises or gashes adorn his beautiful face. I hope he stops fighting. He has so much more to offer if he'd submit to being vulnerable for half a second. Instead, he speaks with his fists—which makes my stomach queasy.

Wait. Why am I worrying about him? I bet he acts like this when he's having a bad hair day.

The voice in the back of my head scolds me, "You know him better than that. Say what you want, Gina, but at the end of the day it matters to you what happens to this man."

I beat the emotional part of my brain back into whatever dark corner of my mind she crawled out from. The feeling that she's right recedes with her. I push myself off the wall and take a couple of steps toward the man in front of me.

"Peter? What's wrong?" Okay, she's not in a closet after all. I was going to say something mean, but my words changed when they hit my tongue.

Fricken invisa-Gina and her empathy. She's going to get our heart ripped out.

"No, it won't."

I make a growly sound in the back of my throat while extending my fingers at my sides, stretching them as far as they'll go.

"Shut up already!"

Yeah, oops. I said that out loud.

"I didn't speak yet." Pete's brows draw together. "Are you okay?"

"I, yeah…" I pause and it finally hits me. "Wait. Are you here to take me away again?" A sour sense of dread swirls inside of me. I don't want my ass hauled off to Ferro mansion. I don't want to leave this place and my new life so soon.

"No, that's not why I stopped by." His gaze is downcast, staring at his boots. "I just thought I'd come over and spend some time with my... friend." Pete looks up with a sad smile on his face. He stares me up and down. "You look good, Gina."

I so desperately want to put a smile on his face that I do a little twirl, kicking up a foot behind me and pretending to primp hair that is still neatly tucked in my bandana.

"I've improved on the bunny slippers," I say lightly. "You like my new look?"

"Yes," he hesitates. I drop my arms and the goofy look on my face slides away when he meets my gaze. "But it's more than that. When I came down those stairs, you looked... happy."

I close the distance between us and hook my elbow with his. I lead us toward the stairs, and we both sit down, side by side, on the steps.

"Thank you. I am happy. Hey, can you believe I did a 10-foot stage dive tonight?"

Pete turns his head slightly. He looks at me from the corner of his eyes and smirks, a small teasing glint wanting to light up.

"Did you trip on another rug while trying to seduce someone?"

"Jerk," I tease, slapping him on the arm, but glad to see a light in his eyes. "You're not supposed to mention that to me ever again. And no, it was intentional and unbelievable."

He takes my hand and stares at it, his finger playing with my now barren ring finger. His smile disappears. Something is eating away at him tonight, and I wish I knew how I could make it better.

"Pete, you said you wanted to talk to me, so talk." I reach over and push his shoulder with my fist, I suppose like a guy would do with his buddy. It feels totally awkward. I put my hand back in my lap. "Let me guess. Sorority girl problems? Are they cat fighting over you? Don't know which one to choose? If you ask me, the pretty blond with the cutout sequined dress looked nice. She had a huge rack and we know how much you like the boobage."

Pete's eyes shoot up to meet mine and fill with regret. He didn't expect me to know about his sorority powwow in the sky. He opens his mouth to talk, but I lift a finger to his lips and cut him off.

"Don't look at me like that, Pete. I'm going to find out about these things. I can't pretend I'm okay with any of it, but can we at least be honest with each other? Like friends?"

He releases my hand and stands up, backing away, his skin turning green like he's going to be sick.

"I need to go—this was a mistake."

He only makes it down the two first steps when I call out to him. "Wait, Pete! Didn't you want to come upstairs and talk?"

Pete looks up the stairwell, leading to my apartment and then back down, shaking his head.

"I'll see you next week at the merger gala. I'll be the guy in the tux, saving a broken-hearted woman from the public eye."

"I'll be there, freshly dumped and ready to be saved."

Pete's crooked grin is half-hearted, but it's there. Without another word, he walks down the stairs and leaves.

YOU CLEAN UP WELL

August 31st , 5:42pm

Another weekend, another party, but this one holds the promise of massive heartburn. As my eyes sweep the breathtaking circular ballroom, a chill runs down my spine. THIS is where high-society will swoon and gossip over the budding romance between poor broken-hearted Regina Granz and the reforming Pete Ferro. The premise of the party? We'll celebrate the official merger of Granz Textiles into Ferro Corp, two families coming together in the name of good business transactions. It just so happens the two young heirs of those families will fall deeply in love and get married. It's a cute story when you don't know all the ugly, underlying details like arson, manslaughter, and blackmail.

Guests are mingling, sipping cocktails, eating hors d'oeuvres, chatting and laughing away in the lush surroundings. Large windows, extravagantly dressed in golden velvets line the far end of the room and frame two large crystal chandeliers. At the front of the room, a screen is hung next to a lectern for the big announcement.

The expansive room is quickly filling with an ungodly amount of nosy guests, all ready to greet me with their consolations. A seed has been planted, and the gossip vine is growing wild. Almost everyone here is now aware that Anthony dumped my ass, and I'm in a state of distraught misery. Having your romantic woes publicly displayed is an excruciating experience. I want to be the girl I was last weekend, the audacious one meeting new people and taking chances. This crowd sucks my boldness dry. I wish Jenny would take over, and shock the Botox out of everyone. But as entertaining as it would be for me, it would also land me a one-way ticket to jail.

So I wait. The next step of the plan is for Pete Ferro to come in and sweep me off of my feet.

It seems like the entire Ferro clan is here tonight, right down to the cousins skulking about the bar and surveying their prospects of getting laid. There's still no sign of Pete. He's probably busy shagging the lady at the coat check or showing the barmaid the proper way to shake his mantini. Despite my initial sarcastic thoughts, I hope he shows up soon, so I know he's okay. He seemed off when I saw him outside Ricky's apartment, and I'm worried. I don't want to be, but I am. Pete was acting so strangely.

People walk past me, exchanging greetings and pleasantries. I'm considering poking my eye out with a fork. It'll be better than hearing one more person's false condolences about Anthony. I shift through the maze of people, heading toward the front entrance. I need some air. I never make it out of the room.

The main doors swing open before I can ascend the staircase, and a handsome man enters the ballroom. He's wearing a tailored black tuxedo, black tie, white button-down shirt and a black vest under his jacket. For once, Peter Ferro doesn't exude arrogance and overconfidence. His posture is impeccably erect, his gaze bright and open. He radiates sophistication and elegance. He also looks adorably anxious and sinfully edible. He seems just as nervous as I am.

I consciously shut my mouth to avoid slipping in a puddle of drool. People standing near me notice the change in my behavior and follow my eyes to Pete. I don't care if everyone sees me gawking. This is what we're here to do after all, make people believe we're in love at first sight, so I gaze as freely as I want.

His sapphire eyes scan the room. When they meet my eyes he smiles warmly and my heart thuds harder inside my chest.

Pete walks toward me and my palms turn clammy. Why does this feel like something new? We've been through so much together already, but today feels different. Today, it feels like we're caught in a fairytale, seeing each other for the first time after the magical spell breaks.

Pete walks toward me, multiple people sidetracking him, wanting to shake his hand and clap him on the shoulder. It's funny what becoming the sole heir to a massive fortune will do to people. A couple of weeks ago, these people wouldn't have given him the time of day. In fact, they'd have run the other way to avoid him at all costs, scared they might lose their teeth--or their wives, for that matter. That threat is still there, but now he has the power that accompanies his name. These people want to be on good terms with those holding power.

It's all part of a nauseating game to gain more money and more power. I know this crowd; they're old money, working out of boredom, instead of necessity.

Pete exchanges brief smiles and nods, still moving determinedly in my direction. Women walk up to him, with the occasional discreet grope, but he just smiles curtly and keeps on walking, shaking off their advances politely.

By the time he reaches me, I've regained most of my composure, but my heart is still slamming in my chest, shocked at his transformation. He looks respectable in his own right. It's a strange and wonderful sight to behold.

When Pete gets within a step of me, his intoxicating scent fills my head. His aftershave probably comes from the same Venetian shop where he orders his fancy body wash. He puts his hands in his pockets, rocks back on his heels and looks down shyly. He behaves like a kid asking a girl to dance for the first time. It's boyish and totally endearing.

"You clean up well, Ferro." I tease, but I mean every word.

He's beautiful. Cleanly shaven, hair still a rumpled mess, but in contrast with the stern lines of the suit it makes him look dashing. There's no other word for it.

He looks up, smirking, his dimple even cuter without his usual facial scruff.

"You clean up well, too, Granz." He winks and then his eyes travel up and down my body, making frequent stops at the draping, low cut front.

I swat his arm with my little black clutch.

"Quit staring down my dress. We both know I'm flat and you're a boob man." I place my hand over my chest, ensuring my little black dress isn't revealing anything to him.

Erin chose my dress, and it's way out of my comfort zone. It's backless, which means I couldn't wear a bra underneath, and the front drapes down into a low "V" shape, halfway down my torso. I'm relying heavily on fashion tape to keep the silky fabric pressed firmly against my skin and my girls hidden away from prying eyes. At least it has flutter sleeves--my shoulders are safe from scandal.

Pete's gaze darkens. He leans in and whispers in my ear. "You've got me wrong, Granz. I'm not a boob man, although I can appreciate a beautifully sculpted set like yours, especially in a dress like that." He pulls away with a serene smile on his face. Curiosity gets the better of me.

"Then what are you? Legs? Ass? Shoulders?" When he doesn't answer, I add, "Toes. You're a toe man. I knew it."

"I think this conversation is a little too intimate for a first meeting," Pete says, laughing lightly.

People are watching, and I'm sure some geriatric has his hearing aide turned way up to catch our conversation. I plaster a prim smile on my lips and nod. My cheeks turn rosy, which is just a bonus. I hear a few older women point it out. Why they equate blushing with purity is beyond me. I'm about as pure as the snow in New Jersey, but compared to Kitty Bang-Bang, I'm a saint. It makes me wonder where I truly fall on the sex scale.

Pete notices my mind is racing. He steps forward and places his hand on my shoulder, smoothing his thumb under the hem of my tiny sleeve. He leans in close.

"You look beautiful tonight," he murmurs, brushing his lips against my cheek as he pulls away.

It catches me so off guard that I gasp. No one hears it but Pete.

I can't look him in the eye, so I move in to straighten his tie. I'm too close, a breath away from his cheek, one hand resting on his chest and the other tugging at his tie.

"So, how are people going to believe I'm the one who cleaned up your act when you show up looking like this?" I speak softly, smoothing my hands over the lapels of his jacket, then step back to assess my work. His eyebrows scrunch together in the center like he doesn't understand.

"I just thought I was supposed to be the one affecting you this way," I say, motioning to his appearance.

Pete looks down at me. His smile disappears, and his eyes search mine intently. Gently, he brushes a finger across my cheek.

"What makes you think that you're not, Gina?"

The smile falls from my face and shatters on the floor. The air has been sucked from my lungs. My lips part and I try to speak, but words don't come.

Someone calls Pete's name. He turns to see who it is, nods toward them and walks away into the crowd, leaving me alone. What the hell? How can he have such a profound effect on me? It's like he chose the perfect string of words, words I want to believe. They fall from his lips like petals without malice, but they cut me all the same. If he's lying, his words knocked the air out of my lungs because he hit me where it hurts most. If he's telling the truth, then I can't even fathom what that means. I'm left in a jumbled mess of confusion, watching his broad shoulders recede into the crowd.

NOT SO LOW-PROFILE EYE CANDY

August 31st , 5:56pm

I watch Pete roam around the room, mingling, occasionally pointing in my direction and talking about me. He's playing his part well. The game is on; that's all it is. An illusion. He's letting people know that I've caught his interest. Women walk up to him, their hands slithering all over him, but he gently and politely detaches them and walks away.

Eventually, my parents arrive and Mom joins me in my corner of solitude, taking the seat next to me. She looks elegant and beautiful as always, but I can see the fatigue in her eyes. Dad walks the opposite direction, straight to Mr. and Mrs. Ferro.

"You look beautiful, Mom." She does. She's wearing a charcoal gray silk dress. It has a flowing skirt adorned with crystals in just the right places. They catch the light when she moves, giving her an ethereal look. The family diamonds are around her neck, in her hair, and on her hands. Her earrings are small and understated. They were her mothers. I bet she had to fight Daddy to wear those tonight.

"Thank you." She smiles and touches my shoulder, gesturing toward my dress. "You are a vision, Regina. This gown is classic with a sultry flare, and you wear it so well." She says the words as if she were proud of me for not dressing like my normal prudish self.

"How's Daddy?" I glance across the room. "Does he still hate me?"

"He doesn't hate you, sweetie. He loves you very much. Just between you and me, he felt horrible for kicking you out. He locked himself in his study and cried for hours after you left. He still cries at night, when he thinks I'm sleeping."

That surprises me. "He cries?"

"Like a colicky baby in a wet diaper." She smiles at me. "Don't tell him I told you that, though, you'll wound his male pride. He'll come around, don't worry. He misses his little girl, and I think that he knows, deep down, that he's partly to blame for all of this mess. He may never say it out loud, but he is sorry. You just need to give him time; this isn't easy for him either. He's lost his family's company. He never saw it coming; you did, and he chose not to listen to you. That's not an easy thing to admit publicly. Let him come to grips with his mistakes. When the time is right, he'll apologize in his way. Now, come with me. The Gambinos have arrived, and I want to welcome them."

Mom and I walk across the lavish ballroom toward Congressman and Mrs. Gambino. I slow down and stop my mother when I see a familiar face standing next to them. It can't be. My heart starts to race, and my mind goes around the multitude of scenarios trying to explain how this can be happening.

"Uh. Mom? Who's that man standing with the Gambinos?"

"What do you mean?" Mother looks at me curiously and then understanding flashes across her face. "Oh, I suppose you haven't seen their son in a long time. That's Philip. He just came back from an extended trip to Europe."

My jaw drops. It's Phil, the good-looking skydiver who kissed me at the party. That guy is Philip Gambino? The Congressman's son? Holy shit, I'm so screwed! When I get home tonight, I am going to KILL Erin for not telling me this important bit of information when she introduced us. She had to know! He's supposed to be my somewhat-meaningless flirt, my low-profile eye-candy, my little indulgence before I go on a lifelong diet of nunnery. Fuckity-fuck-fucker-fuck! I can't have him in the same room as Pete, especially not with all the media here.

Constance will kill me!

"What is it darling?" Mom senses my distress and follows my gaze. A whole other level of understanding crosses her face. "Oh. OH! Oh, dear. Well, this is somewhat awkward."

She places a hand on her mouth in attempted disapproval, but then gets a proud Mommy look on her face. Suddenly, she's glowing with pride.

"Mom!" I elbow her gently.

From the corner of my eye, I see Pete shift at the far end of the room. My eyes go to him briefly. He glances at me, a look of concern flashes across his face and he takes a step forward. My hand gesture is discreet, but I send him the message to stay away. I need to figure out how I'm going to handle this.

"I must say, between Peter Ferro and Philip Gambino, my shy daughter has become quite the catch. You have great taste in men, darling." My mother giggles like a hormonal teenager, which leaves me gaping like a docked fish. "Oh, what a delicious pickle to be in! How long have you and Philip, you know," she drops her voice to a loud whisper and places her hand next to her mouth to hide her words from lip-readers, "been having in-ter-course?" She says intercourse slowly, breaking it up into three long, painful syllables.

My eyes bug out of my head, and I try not to screech. I tug on my Mom's hand and try to pull her in the opposite direction, but she won't budge.

"What? No! Mom, it's not like that. We kissed once at a party in Erin's building. He doesn't know who I am, and probably won't even recognize me. I looked so different."

I knew Erin used to be friends with Philip Gambino before she left home, but I never realized they had kept up with their friendship. I thought I was her only tie to her former life. Why the hell didn't she tell me?

"Well, then," Mom says taking my hand. "Let's get this over with."

We continue our walk toward the Gambinos. We politely say our greetings and exchange meaningless pleasantries, but Philip is engaged in conversation with someone else and doesn't look our way. When Congressman Gambino claps Philip on the back to get his attention, I look down.

"Son, you remember Mrs. Granz and her daughter, Regina, don't you?"

My eyes are studiously fixed on Phil's polished black leather shoes peeking out from his perfectly pressed charcoal gray slacks. Maybe he won't recognize me. He'd had a few drinks at the party, he was jet-lagged, and it was late. Plus, I looked completely different and I introduced myself as Gina, not Regina. I chance a glance at him and that friendly smile of his greets me. He's wearing a designer suit and looks stunning in it. His hair is still in need of a cut, but it looks perfect on him. It lets that thrill seeking, skydiving side of him show through his refined attire and demeanor.

"It's a pleasure to see you again, Regina." He extends a hand, and I take it. He drops a small kiss on the top of my hand just as he did at the party. He looks up briefly, his eyebrows furrowed, and I do my best not to squirm.

"Well," Mom begins, gesturing toward the Gambinos, "why don't we get our drinks refreshed and let these kids get reacquainted?" She ushers Mr. and Mrs. Gambino away, leaving us alone, but not before giving me a wink and a not so discreet thumbs up as she goes. OMG. Someone shoot me. This can't be my life. My Mom is giving me a thumbs up because she thinks I have a new sex buddy.

"So, Regina. It's been a while. What have you been up to?" He asks, dropping my hand. Maybe he doesn't recognize me after all.

"School mostly." I'm usually good at small talk, but this is not a usual scenario. I look everywhere except at Phil. I'm silently praying that he doesn't make the connection. Honestly, he'd have to have a few loose brain hemispheres to not recognize me, but a girl can hope. He had to have hit the ground a couple of times jumping off of stages and out of planes. One good shot to the head could result in a sucky memory.

My eyes keep going to Pete, who is leaning back against the bar, sipping a tumbler of something that looks strong. Some guy, probably a younger cousin of his, based on the resemblance, is talking to him, but Pete's looking directly at me.

"So, how was your econometrics quiz yesterday morning? Did you try to show off some bra to earn extra points as I suggested?"

I'm still caught in Pete's mesmerizing gaze, but I shake my head slightly.

"Uh, no, I-I didn't have to. The quiz went well." It takes a while, but when I realize what he just asked, my stomach drops into my stilettos. Oh, shit!

My head whips to look at Phil and his smile widens. He does recognize me. At the party, I'd complained about my upcoming quiz and he'd suggested I show some cleavage to get a better grade. Being the well-mannered lady I am, I give him an exaggerated wave, nudge him with my elbow and say with way too much volume and enthusiasm, "Talk about a coinkydink, huh?"

COINKYDINK? Oh, God! I'm such a dork! My fake smile is going to make my face crack, and I probably look like a clown. Or an ass. Or an ass wearing a clown costume. Philip laughs and places his empty glass on a nearby table.

"Well I, for one, couldn't be more pleased with this turn of events."

I open my mouth to talk. He looks optimistic, like this is a good thing. Under normal circumstances, I'd be ecstatic. Who wouldn't be? Our parents are friends. We both run in the same social circles. I like him. He likes me. Under normal circumstances we would be a great match, but I need to let him know this thing between us can't happen.

The flirting was fun, but I can't let myself get into a public relationship of any kind with Philip Gambino. If we are seen in public together, it's bound to get splattered all over the tabloids. Connie will have my head mounted on one of those suits of armor that I've seen in the halls of the Ferro mansion. This goes against her plan.

Phil cuts me off before I get to say anything by putting a finger over my lips.

"Don't feel guilty. I understand why you didn't tell me who you really are. I did the same thing, remember? I made Erin promise never to tell anyone about my family and by the look on your face, I'm guessing she's still holding true to that promise. Believe me, I totally get it."

And the crazy thing is, he really does get it. He probably hides who he is from everyone so that they'll like him for who he is--not for his connections or his money.

He places a hand on my lower back, directly on my skin. The touch is warm and soft, and I would love to enjoy it, but apprehension is consuming me. My eyes scan the room, trying to find Mrs. Ferro, hoping she isn't plotting my demise over this, but she's busy going over documents with my father. In the whole room, only Pete is following my every move, sipping his drink and observing from a distance.

Phil guides us toward the tables. My legs are so shaky that I follow willingly. I need to sit down in the worst possible way, and I have to set things straight with Phil.

"Philip, about the party, you have to understand that this," I gesture between the two of us. He cuts me off again, taking my hand in his.

"I do understand, don't worry. You've just been through a horrible breakup with your ex-fiancé. Everybody's heard about it. My mother hasn't stopped talking about it since I got back from Europe. You were out looking for a fun rebound. It happens. If that's what you need, that's what I'll be. No pressure. It's okay to just have fun and forget about everyone else. We'll see where things go from there, okay?"

He's so sweet and gentlemanly, but this can't go anywhere and I can't tell him why. It's not fair.

We arrive at a table, and he pulls out a chair for me. As I sit down, a loud screech of feedback comes over the sound system. All eyes turn toward the front of the room where my parents and Pete's parents stand together behind the lectern. Mrs. Ferro stands directly behind the microphone and starts to make her announcement. Her voice has that false warmth that is classic Constance.

"I thank you all for coming here this evening in honor of Ferro Corp's expansion. We are proud to announce the Granz Textiles merger into Ferro Corp as one of our new sister companies. Together, our two companies will bring life to exciting new products that will make a difference worldwide, from the fashion industry to the medical field."

She goes on to discuss the future of Granz Textiles, now that it is in the hands of Ferro Corp, and all the wondrous things they will accomplish. A business executive takes over the presentation, explaining the many colorful graphs and charts flashing across the screen next to the lectern.

My Dad is visibly holding back his anger, and my mother holds his hand, keeping him somewhat restrained. Phil discreetly holds my hand under the table the entire time. I'm a jumbled mess of nerves, wondering if anyone has x-ray vision and sees the small physical connection going on under the linens.

As the executive finishes his presentation, Mrs. Ferro takes the microphone once more to finish her well-scripted speech.

"As a symbol of the merger between the Ferro and Granz families, I would like to ask my son, Peter, and Miss Regina Granz to join us at the front."

What the…?

Most eyes are on Pete, for which I am eternally grateful, but people who actually know who I am, turn around and gesture for me to stand and go to the front of the room. God, I hate this.

Phil lets go of my hand and pulls out my chair, giving me a little shove and saying in my ear, "Go on, Gina. Just try not to sing. I don't think my ears can take an encore." He smirks and I elbow him in the side. Why does he have to be so perfect?

I stand and take a couple shaky steps toward the front of the room, but when I see Pete already standing there, waiting for me, my nerves dissolve, and my stride becomes more confident.

We're a team now, friends. As much as my mother was there, standing proudly by my father's side while he was publicly humiliated by having his company engulfed by a mega-corporation, Pete and I need to do this together. He's there waiting for me.

I can't let him or my family down.

When I reach the front of the room, I stand in front of Pete, my back to him, and he places his hands on my hips. He lowers his mouth to my ear and whispers, "I've been watching you all evening. You're trembling like a leaf, and you look green. Are you feeling ill?"

I turn my head to the side and reply, "C'mon, Mr. Poet, say it like you mean it. Will I soon be blowing chunks? The answer is yes."

Pete silently chuckles. His chest is pressed against my back, and I can feel his laugh vibrate.

"Don't worry, I've got you, Jenny," and his fingers squeeze my hips.

That makes me laugh. I place a hand on one of his and press gently before letting go. His grip on me is reassuring and gives me the strength to stand up tall.

"Now," Mrs. Ferro says, continuing her speech, "let us clear the floor while Peter and Regina share the first waltz of the evening."

WHAT THE WALTZ?
August 31st , 6:31pm

WHAT?!

Our parents move away from the lectern, my mother stroking my father's back reassuringly. Pete walks over to the DJ, leaving me stranded alone at the front of the room looking like an idiot, tapping my fingers on my thighs. He and the DJ exchange a couple of words, gesturing with their hands and nodding.

Pete removes his jacket, vest, tie and cufflinks, setting them on the DJ's table. When he comes back, he unbuttons the top button of his shirt and rolls his cuffs midway up his forearms, the whole time looking straight at me with those blue bedroom eyes.

When he's ready, he walks over and offers his hand. I slip my hand in his while he rests his other hand on my waist. He tips his head down to look into my eyes.

"Ready to have your ass kicked, Granz?" The corner of his mouth lifts to one side. His goading breaks my unease.

"Kick my ass? At a waltz? I'm a ballerina, dude! We waltz in our sleep! We'll see whose ass gets whipped." Pete grins at my words and I realize what I said. "Shut up and dance, Ferro."

Pete bursts out laughing and the music starts. Glenn Miller's trombone rings out a few notes of warning and Pete's mischievous smile says the rest. Oh, crapsticks! He intends on swing dancing instead of waltzing, and I'm not wearing the right clothing!

"Uh, Pete?" I tug on his shoulder. "Easy on the lifts, okay? I can't flash my undies to anyone here tonight."

"As you wish, Miss Granz." His words are coupled with a wink, and my hopes go the way of the Titanic. Crap. He's totally planning on showing everyone the color of my panties.

Before I can back out, he spins me out, away from him and quickly snaps me back. The movement propels me so that I crash into his chest, and I'm eye-level with his exposed neck. God, he smells good. What is that? Leather? The guy smells like a saddle and spices. The little dip at the base of his throat is just begging to be licked.

We freeze for a couple of beats, smiling at each other, and when the intro fades into the melody, he starts leading me into the dance that I taught him. Our steps are perfectly synchronized and lively. He leads me across the dance floor, making me move in any way he wants. His grip is firm and authoritative. He isn't a weak dance partner, and it's not because I'm being a good girl and following perfectly.

When I try to take control, his grip on me tightens and he guides me more forcefully, pushing me under his arm, spinning me out, and snapping me back. We're breathing hard and the rush is amazing. I forget the people watching. It's just us and the magical pulse of the trumpet. The singer's voice is lush and spot on. It's like we're lost in time, pulled apart from the things that threaten to destroy us. It's just me and Pete, our feet moving perfectly together.

"And you thought dancing was for pussies." I echo back the words he said so long ago.

He pushes me out, leads me under his arm, and then brings both arms down encircling me. We're nose-to-nose, both of us breathing hard. "You changed my mind."

Before I can answer, he spins me out again.

Pete's being a good boy, avoiding any lifts, but he has that devilish look about him. Pete's holding back, and it's killing him. It's also killing me because sooner or later, he's going to surprise me with a flip and my ass, clad in cheeky Brazilian-cut undies, will grace the cover of gossip magazines everywhere.

A few more bars of music go by, and we're face-to-face, both smiling and breathing hard.

I jerk his wrist and say, "It's my turn to lead, Ferro. Try and keep up."

Pete nods, agreeing to let me take the lead for a while. I try a more complex step and Pete fumbles, his toes stepping on mine. We both stop dancing and laugh, never letting go of each other's hands.

Between breathy giggles, I say, "I'm totally kicking your ass."

Pete grins, his eyes never leaving mine. Longer strands of hair flop down on his forehead, almost reaching his eyes, and he flips his hair back with a chuckle.

"Yes, you are. You'll have to teach me some more of those moves someday."

"How about now? Let's try it slowly." I slow down our tempo by half. Pete looks down at my feet and studies my moves, then concentrates on his own. We repeat the move over and over again until he gets it. "Ready for double time?"

Pete answers by taking over the lead, doing the same step but at the proper speed. It amazes me how good he is at this and how well our styles match. I feel like I'm Ginger Rogers and he's my Fred Astaire; we were meant to dance together.

The song approaches the end, and he hasn't flipped me over or done any lifts. I'm expecting it at any moment. There is no way he's going to pass up such an opportunity.

It's coming, I can feel it. It's the final notes of the song. He spins me in close. My back is pressed against his front. I close my eyes. He guides my arm above my head to turn me around toward him and I drop, arching backward in his arms.

The last note has played. I'm in a dip, his back to the rest of the room. He's hovering close to my face, both of us breathing hard. His body is only inches away from mine. We're in our own private bubble. My hands are clasped around his neck whereas his are on my back, keeping me close.

People start to clap, applauding us. Pete's gaze travels down and up my body, and he grins.

"I thought you said you weren't going to flash anyone tonight?"

I remove one hand from his neck to discreetly check my skirt, making sure it hasn't ridden up too far, but I'm safe. The skirt is flowing down nicely, hiding all the bits I want to keep covered.

"Your eyes deceive you, Mr. Ferro. I'm not flashing anyone." I tease, smiling.

"Really? From here, I have a delectable view. It's a real shame we're just friends." He moistens his lips, and his gaze darkens as it drops back down. It's only when I notice he's staring at my chest that it registers. I feel drafty in places I shouldn't be.

Everything happens so fast, but it feels like slow motion. As soon as I realize my left boob has popped free of my dress – damn fashion tape – my body stiffens and my face flames up.

This isn't happening! I want to curl up into a ball and cry. No, I want to move to another state, get a boob job, change my face and THEN curl up into a ball and cry.

Singing off-key karaoke in front of a bunch of partygoers in a rundown apartment is one thing. Showing my breasts off in the middle of a formal business affair, surrounded by the most influential people in New York City is another.

My eyes start to prickle and my view of Pete blurs under a watery film of unshed tears. I repeatedly blink, trying desperately not to cry in public.

Pete's cockiness changes to reassurance. "Don't worry, no one can see you but me. You're fine." His voice is soft and kind.

He pulls me close to him, hiding me from everyone so I can adjust my dress, but before I succeed, we hear rapid clicking. A wave of unrelenting flashes of light blinds us both.

TESTOSTERONE
August 31st , 6:38pm

What was a happy moment of dancing turns into a nightmare. Within the next few minutes, the pictures will be uploaded to the Internet and the entire world will see me exposed while cradled in Pete Ferro's arms. Oh, God.

I cover my eyes, and Pete straightens us both into a standing position, keeping me close to him the entire time. He discreetly fixes my top, but the tips of his fingers gently brush up against my nipple. I suck in a jagged breath as my stomach stirs at the unexpected touch.

Pete's muscles cord tightly as the clicking and flashes of light continue. When I look up, his jaw is clenched, and the little vein on the side of his temple looks like a fire hose. He's staring down the group of photographers next to us. Pete looks down at me, making certain that I'm decent again, then releases me. Before I know it, he's charging toward the small group of photographers. He doesn't ask; he just starts yanking the cameras away from them.

Guests are gasping. Some of the Ferro men from the other end of the reception hall are laughing. One of them walks over. He doesn't have the trademark Ferro blue eyes, but he looks like them—angular features with dark hair and the Ferro stance that says he knows his place in the world, and it's right on top.

"Pete," he says walking toward his cousin.

Peter turns and growls. "Not now Bryan. Go back to your mother." As Pete speaks, he grabs another camera from unsuspecting hands.

"Hey! I was invited here to photograph the party. If you don't like it, then take it up with your mother." The photographer is bold as he says it, but then Pete turns on him, livid. The guy shrinks back and disappears into his wrinkled Sears suit.

Peter grabs his collar and pulls him so they're nose to nose. The muscles in Pete's neck are corded tight.

"That's right. You're here to photograph the party, not embarrass my friend, but that's exactly what you're doing. Leave now, or I'll make you leave. Your equipment will be returned if you comply. If you don't walk away, I won't be so kind." Pete is slowly lifting the guy off the ground as he speaks, then drops him.

The photographers that have been stripped of their cameras stand there stunned. A few walk away without a word, unwilling to lose thousands of dollars of equipment, while others stand their ground. It's those people that worry me.

Pete grabs another camera, ripping it from the man's hands. The next fellow isn't so lucky. When he fails to hand it over, Pete describes exactly what he plans to do to him, and it's not pretty. He reaches for the camera and jerks it away.

I can't let him do this. I'm nobody. My puny boob and I will be yesterday's news in no time; there's really nothing to see anyway. Pete, on the other hand, is a whole other ballgame. Pictures and videos of this fight will be plastered everywhere, and I know what his hands can do. I don't want him to be the cause of another tragedy, especially not on my account.

"Try and take it, Ferro."

Pete's fingers ball into fists. The guy refuses to hand over his camera. Pete refuses to make it look like a struggle. The fastest way to take something you want is a fist to the face. The veins in his neck are ready to pop. He's going in for a swing. If I don't act now, the photographer's face will be pudding. I run.

Pete pulls his arm back, ready to punch, and I squeeze myself between him and the photographer. The man is a little taller than me and taken by surprise. Everything happens in rapid succession, too fast to tell what would happen next.

"Don't!" My voice leaves me in a rush as something hard crashes into my cheek. For a second I think it's Pete's fist, but it's cold and hard. I blink once and touch my hand to my cheek. Holy shit. It was the camera.

The photographer turns pale and steps away from me. He took a swing at Pete and hit me instead. I ran right into his fist with his camera still attached. The guy keeps stepping back, hands up, trying to apologize.

"I didn't mean to hit her. She ran right into me. I swear to God!"

Pete is seeing red. His gaze narrows as his jaw locks. He's done talking. Pete rips the camera off the guy's hand and throws it. The equipment goes flying through the air and then crashes to the floor. The glass in the lens shatters on contact.

Everyone is watching. Cameras are clicking. Cell phones are recording. And the scariest monster of all is making a beeline directly for her son. Constance

Ferro has a look on her face that could castrate an army.

This has to stop now. Before the crazy cousins jump in, because they're headed this way too. The entire family is going to get into a brawl over my boob. It's like a flash mob—a real one. This will ruin the merger, destroy my parents, and slaughter Pete's image in the process.

I move without thinking, just wanting this to stop.

"STOP! PETE! DON'T!" I rush between them again and reach for his arm. "STOP!"

For a fraction of a second, I'm the target of his wrath. It's both beautiful and frightening all at once. All pure, raw emotion with nothing held back. His crystal blue eyes, normally filled with flirty amusement, cloud with hatred and hurt. His hands, normally gentle and sensual, are clenched tightly into weapons.

My arms fly up, instinctively protecting my face in case he doesn't have time to pull back his punch.

Nothing happens. I don't see stars and I'm not plastered against the ballroom floor. I chance a peek. His fist is still up in the air, but he's stopped his swing, holding it there.

"Gina, get out of the way." Pete says through clenched teeth. His whole body is trembling with the effort of holding himself back, his eyes focused on the man behind me.

"No, Peter. I can't let you do this. Let it go. Please!"

"I won't let these sons of bitches do this to you."

Stepping closer, I rest my hands firmly on his chest, gently pushing him back.

"It's okay, Peter. It's not worth it." I'm begging now and mouth the word, 'please.'

Pete lowers his fist and looks at me, not understanding. He takes a step back and turns around, running his hand through his hair. He stomps his foot down and lets out a frustrated growl-like scream before punching the air. My shoulders slump in relief. He's letting out steam, but I still have work to do. I need to get rid of dipstick behind me before Pete pounds his ass into the floor.

Turning to the stunned photographer, I see him reach for his camera on the ground. He squeals like a girl as I stab his hand with the heel of my stiletto.

"I just saved your face, asshole, now you're going to save mine. Forget the camera and LEAVE!"

His fingers stretch, trying to reach once more for the camera, and I twist my heel further into his hand, making him whimper and cry out in pain. I remove my foot from his hand.

"You two deserve each other," he mutters angrily. "Pair of fucking lunatics." He scrambles for the exit, leaving the camera behind.

You don't know the half of it, buddy.

But my victory is short lived. Pete is still trying to come to grips with his anger, and I have to make sure he won't do anything he'll regret later. His mother parts the crowd of onlookers like it's the Red Sea.

"Peter Ferro." She says his name like she's scolding a toddler.

I cut in front of her and take Pete by the arm. "Lovely party, Mrs. Ferro. The most exciting I've been to in ages. I'm certain news of your merger will be sprawled across the front of every newspaper in the country by morning. Odds are HuffPo already has something up." I talk swiftly and with confidence I don't feel. "If you'll excuse us."

Walking up to Pete, I place a firm hand on his shoulder. He's so on edge that he flinches upon contact.

"Pete, follow me." He looks up.

His face is a tangled mess of emotions; I can't tell what's going on in his head, but he does as I say and takes my hand. I need to move him away from the crowd. Too many people are watching us; among those people are a protective brother, pissed off cousins, and a mother that's growing horns.

When we get to a remote corner of the room, I push through a set of doors that lead to the stairwell. There's someone sneaking a smoke. There's a no smoking policy in this place and from the looks of it, this waiter can't afford a fine. He flinches and I smile at him.

"I won't tell if you don't."

"Done." He puts out his cigarette and nods. "I wasn't here and I have no idea where Peter Ferro is. If you'll excuse me." The waiter walks past us and back into the ballroom.

We're finally alone.

"Are you all right?"

I start to ask him more, but a tap on my shoulder interrupts me. Pete looks over my shoulder and scowls. I turn around. It's Philip.

"Gina, are you okay? What the hell happened out there?" He places both his hands on my shoulders. Oddly, I don't want him touching me in front of Pete. It feels wrong. I politely remove his hands and let go of him, but he holds my hands tighter, possessively.

"Just a wardrobe malfunction. Some photographers got a good view. No biggie." I'm downplaying it. It is a huge deal for me, but I don't want to get Pete all riled up again.

Phil sighs, "Damn those fuckers, always trying to get their shots." He nods toward Pete. "Thanks for looking out for her out there."

I look between the two men, utterly confused. Phil is still holding my hands and Pete's eyes zone in on the simple touch. He releases one hand and lifts my chin up with a finger to study my face.

"What happened here?" Pete tenses beside me, and it's only then I notice the throbbing pain on my right cheek. When I press my fingers to it, they come back wet. I'm bleeding. Great.

"I got in the way of a flying projectile. When cameras have wings, right? Or is that pigs?" I shrug, hoping to not make a big deal out of it, but Pete turns his back to me like he can't stand to look at my battered face.

I can't figure out why he behaved the way he did. The old Pete would have posed for the camera. The new one went Godzilla on their asses.

"Let me get something for that cut," Phil says, removing his finger from my chin. "I'll be right back." He drops a small kiss on my uninjured cheek. I nod, and Phil heads toward the bar.

"So. You and Gambino, huh? Was he the reason you were so happy last week?" Pete says.

I turn toward Pete. He's leaning up against the wall, hands in his pockets. I shake my head and take a step closer to him.

"No. Yes. No. You know as well as I do that a relationship between me and Phil isn't possible." I look back at the fire door, wondering when he'll be back. I kind of wanted some time alone with Pete.

"He's a good man, Gina. Clean cut, good looking, from a good family with good values, well educated, promising career and the way he looks at you..."

My mouth quirks up to one side. I can't help but tease him.

"Wow, you paint a pretty picture of him. Do you have a crush perhaps, Ferro? I don't think you're Phil's type." It's meant as a joke, to get a rise out of him, but his face remains somber.

"No, but he's most definitely yours."

I got nothing. He's right. Under any other circumstances, Philip would be my type. I like him a lot and, when we talk, it feels natural and right.

Pete and I stay silent for a while, just looking at each other. So many unspoken words beg to come out. I hate that I'm still not free to make my own choices. At the same time, though, Pete has become such a huge part of my life that if it were possible to cut all ties with him, I can't say for certain that I would.

Part of me has grown attached to him somehow. Regina Granz, befriending a ruffian. Odder things have happened, I suppose, like being besties with a 'libertine', as Erin likes to call herself.

Phil comes back with napkins, a glass of water and a plastic baggie filled with ice. When he starts to dab the blood off of my face, I take the napkin from him and do it myself.

Pete pushes himself off the wall and clears his throat. He unrolls his sleeves and buttons the top button of his shirt.

"Now that you're in good hands, I'll leave you two alone." Pete stares Philip up and down. "Hurt her and you'll wish you didn't." His eyes focus on the door that leads to the ballroom and his entire demeanor changes. His lips twitch up into a crooked smile. "Now if you'll excuse me, I saw a long pair of golden legs that need spreading."

My lips curl in disgust. Pete, the player, is back. He pushes past us and walks into the ballroom. We follow him, watching. He heads toward a group of glamorous, high-maintenance, long legged women that have been begging for his attention all evening. He ignored them until now.

For me.

But that's not completely true. A nagging memory reminds me this is all an act. He did it for himself. He made sure this event would be covered in every single media outlet--as efficiently as possible.

Phil puts the ice pack on my cheek, and I suck in air through my teeth like a hiss. A single tear rolls down my cheek. I didn't even realize it was there.

"I'm sorry, did I hurt you?" His voice fills with concern and his thumb brushes my shoulder delicately.

"No, you didn't hurt me. It just stings." I don't lie to him, not really. It does sting.

STREETWALKERS, SPOTLIGHTS, & GOLD DIGGERS

August 31st, 7:05pm

I hate when people fuss over me, but I hate it even more when it's public. Forget trying to go back unnoticed to the party. Mom is pouting because I've kept my swing dancing a secret from her, and everyone else wants to know what sparked the fight between Pete and the photographers. With the way Pete and I were standing, they couldn't see it.

I'm not about to publicly admit I just titty-winked the entire world. They'll find out soon enough anyway. Philip attempts to keep me close to him, draping a protective arm around my shoulders.

I excuse myself from Philip and the other well-meaning guests, pushing my way through the crowd as politely as possible. The last thing I see before finally finding refuge in my usual go-to place -- an empty bathroom stall-- is Pete, wrapped up in multiple female arms.

I sit on the lowered seat cover and let the tears fall for as long as they need to. I cry for Pete, not certain why. I cry for the embarrassment those pictures will bring. I cry for Phillip and our hopeless would-be relationship. I cry for my future empty marriage. I cry because, once again, someone was prettier, better, and smarter than me. It's crushing me. My fake relationship is causing me more grief than a real one.

"I'm so mental," I say to myself. I wipe my tears and stand up. I need to put myself together before I head back out. I step out of the stall, hoping to have a quiet moment to fix myself up, and discover I'm not alone in the restroom.

Constance is waiting for me.

She stands in front of me like a statue. She doesn't lean on the counter or slouch like any normal person would. Even in the bathroom, her posture is perfect. She stares straight at me, cold and unfeeling, as usual.

"Miss Granz, I must both congratulate and reprimand you."

I walk over to the sink and pretend to study my face in the mirror, seemingly unaffected by her presence.

"Oh? Why is that, Mrs. Ferro?"

"Your little act of bravery, breaking up the fight between my son and those photographers, is an outstanding example of what I expect from you in this position. You have courage and strength, and the media will eat it up."

I'm waiting for the other shoe to drop and....

"However,"

Clunk.

"While you are in here having your little moment, young Mr. Gambino is outside this door pacing, worried about you. My son, on the other hand, is gathering up a collection of women, intending to fill the family limousine for a private party. This is not the image I want to be portrayed. Need I remind you what your responsibilities are, Miss Granz?"

"No, you don't." I dab my eyes with a tissue and reapply some liner. "I know perfectly well what my responsibilities are, Mrs. Ferro." When I'm done, I turn to face her.

"Good. Now, I want you to go back out there and do what you are supposed to do." She lifts a perfect eyebrow, "Or you'll wish you had when you had the chance."

I square my shoulders and straighten my back. "Is that a threat, Mrs. Ferro?"

"Yes, it is." Her voice is cold and devoid of emotion. "If I were you, I'd take this threat very seriously. You are in no position to slight me. Don't make me change my good opinion of you. So far you have proven to be trustworthy, but headstrong. Don't think your little act of rebelliousness went unnoticed. When I send someone with a message, I expect you to respond accordingly. I am not a lenient person."

Just when I thought there would be no repercussions from ignoring her message to move into the mansion, out it comes. Her threat sits heavily on my shoulders. She will throw me into jail as easily as one would flick a bug off a shoulder.

"Now, Miss Granz, the next time photographers try to take pictures of you, no matter how revealing or compromising they may be, as long as you are with my son, you let them. They have a job to do and so do you. I suggest you get to it immediately. Go, run to my son and cry in his arms instead of cowering alone in here. It's astounding that you may possibly be the only woman in this entire place who isn't hanging all over him." She eyes me as if I'm broken, incapable of feelings. She adjusts the rings on her finger. They slip on her fingers because of the weight. There's one large ring embossed with the Ferro crest in shiny gold. She turns it back into place with a snap, as if setting a bone, then smiles at me, coolly.

"Regardless, you are going to change that, starting now. Go out there and fall in love with Peter, and make certain that I believe it."

Mrs. Ferro turns to leave. She unlocks the door and barely manages to get it open a crack. I stomp my way behind her and shove the door closed, and lock it again.

Mrs. Ferro turns and I'm in her face. Her only reaction, the only way I have of knowing that I've made some impression on her, is that damned lifted eyebrow.

"Don't you dare," I yell. "I may be the only person in this entire place that actually cares about Peter and what happens to him. You were supposed to have journalists here, professional reporters. Not trashy, gossip rag paparazzi. Those people only want one thing. To drag Pete's reputation farther down the sewers. Who let them in and why didn't you throw them out?"

"I know exactly what those photographers want. That's why I invited them. Don't ever question my methods, Miss Granz. Those photographers were paid to do exactly what they did. To create whatever scandal they could and have both of you right in the middle."

I point to the door that leads to the ballroom.

"You did that on purpose? You set him up to have the press all over him? You knew he'd fight if they got in his face! What would they have done if he actually hit one of them?"

Her lips pull into a thin smile as those Ferro eyes bore into me.

"That was a happy accident. Their directions were to harass you and Peter just enough to get him to protect you. Fate worked in our favor with your," she glances at my dress and then back into my eyes, "faulty attire."

"He's your son! How could you do that to him?"

"I always get what I want. You're a stage performer, are you not?"

I nod, not seeing where this conversation is going.

"Let me make it crystal clear—I've set the stage, the actors are now in place, and we have the audience's rapt attention. The spotlight is now on you. It's your turn to play your part and turn my son around. You can start by getting rid of your new young suitor, dressing more like a socialite and less like a streetwalker, and getting Peter away from that horde of gold-digging women."

I walk back to the counter and rest both palms down, head hanging down between my shoulders. I look up at my reflection in the mirror. It's just me. I'm no powerhouse, no one influential. I'm just plain old Regina Granz, and Peter has already turned me down too many times to count.

"Why does everyone think that I can change him? You can't change someone. They are who they are."

Mrs. Ferro unlocks the door and places her hand on the handle.

"I'm not asking you to change him. I'm ordering you to clean up my family's name by reigning in one of my sons in the public eye. I suggest you do it and I don't care how, so long as you stay away from Philip Gambino."

I turn and rest my hips against the counter. "Really? Another threat? I'm a lucky girl."

She lowers her lashes and examines the audaciously large diamond ring on her left hand. She tilts it to the side, watching the light dance off the massive stone.

"No dear, it's advice. I rarely offer anything of the sort, Miss Granz." She looks up at her reflection in the mirror, smooths her gown, and adds, "If I were you, I'd take it."

Mrs. Ferro walks out of the restroom, letting voices and laughter from the reception echo through the open door. I turn and stare at myself in the mirror again. A swollen gash throbs angrily from my right cheek. My skin is already turning an awesome shade of purple and my eyes are puffy.

Frustrated, I slap both hands on the counter by the sink and yell. I can't change Pete. That's not in my power.

I thought I did. I really thought I did, but people don't change.

Seeing him tonight gave me hope that he'd started to come around, but a nice tuxedo, a suave dance, and a warm smile aren't proof of anything. He puts on a good show, but ultimately the decision to make any real changes is his.

I put myself back together, and I walk out of the restroom, determined to do my part. I make my way back into the ballroom to try and find Pete. How the heck can I get him away from his hoochie horde? My eyes scan the room, but he's nowhere to be found and neither is the tramp troupe for that matter.

I'm too late; he's gone. A pair of hands rests on my shoulders and I feel someone pressing up against my back.

"I've been looking for you. Feeling better?"

It's Phil. His voice is most welcome, and I want to lean into him so badly and let myself be comforted by someone kind, but I can feel Mrs. Ferro's eyes on me. Reluctantly, I wriggle away, breaking any contact from him.

"I'm sorry, Philip, I'm tired. I think I'll just head on home."

Phil's hand reaches up to touch me, but I take a step back.

"I can drive you home if you want."

This guy is everything I've ever wanted and the thought of having him drive me home and what that could lead to is tempting, but I can't. I have to push him away. I take another step back.

"No, that's all right, but thank you. I have a driver waiting for me."

He smiles at me and stuffs his hands in his pockets. "Another time then?"

I nod, not wanting to tell him this can never happen. "Another time."

Another lifetime.

POPCORN AND REALITY TV
September 11th, 7:31pm

A week and a half worth of newspapers and magazines stare mockingly at me from their stack on the coffee table. I think I can die miserably now. My popped boob and I made every paper, magazine and trashy gossip website imaginable. More cameras went off than the ones right around us. The place was flooded with photographers we didn't even notice.

Most printed publications were blurred out due to censorship laws, but the internet is an unforgiving bitch, and my perky little nip is now more famous than my face. Going to school has been excruciating, knowing that everyone in my class, along with my professors, have probably seen the pictures.

Not a single article depicts Pete and me as a budding young couple like Constance wanted. Instead, they focus on the fight between Pete and the photographers, my booby-oopsie, and the fact that Pete left with some beautiful rich heiress after being disappointed in the perks that Granz Textiles had to offer.

Since the gala, I've become a hermit. I go to class and come back to the apartment. Phil has been texting and calling me incessantly. He even surprised me on campus in between classes with a hot cup of coffee. I had to make sure my driver was nowhere in sight. Otherwise, he probably would have reported it to Mrs. Ferro. It wouldn't surprise me to discover the car is wired to record sound and video.

And Pete. That's the worst part. I haven't seen him since the gala. He hasn't reached out, and we haven't had any planned public appearances since. A couple of times I punched his number into my phone, wanting to talk to him, just to hear his voice and make sure he's okay.

I even thought about asking if he wanted another dance lesson at the club, but I chickened out and shut off my phone instead. I couldn't face the possibility of his rejection. I never know which side of Pete Ferro I will get, and the thought of being turned down by the player is not something I need right now.

How absurd is that? I'm scared of being rejected by the man who I'll be married to.

"Hey, Gina! It's stripper time! Check it out! Dick got a makeover and he's hubba-hubba-hot tonight!" Erin interrupts my pity party by yanking a magazine from my hands and tossing it on the floor behind the couch.

She shuts off the lights before sitting down next to me and plops the bowl of popcorn on my knees. This has become a nice ritual of ours. Popcorn and real reality TV with my best friend.

The lights are on in the stripper's apartment, and she's practically crawling up the man she's with tonight. Not her usual M.O. She usually saunters in, acting aloof and slightly disinterested, until she starts to pole dance.

Not tonight, though. She's breaking her pattern and wow! She's really going to town with this guy. His hands are all over her, squeezing her ass through her black leather pants, and then running up her back and tangling in her long brown hair. A moment later, he's smoothing those locks down over her sequined gold top.

This isn't frantic or awkward. Dick is all passion and intensity of movement, worshiping every inch of her body, claiming every bit he can manage to touch.

I wonder if they love each other.

The way he's holding her--like he doesn't want to let her go, like she might vanish into thin air--makes me envious. The only person to have ever touched me like that was Pete; that is until he turned me down and walked away.

Blinking twice, I clear my thoughts and look back at the show underway. The stripper brings her hands up to Dick's shoulders and removes his jacket. She tosses it to the side.

"This is weird." Erin says what I'm thinking. "She's breaking all of her rules."

"I know." What the hell is she thinking?

The woman removes his shirt as quickly as she can, their lips breaking contact only long enough to pull Dick's shirt over his head. From what I can see around our soon-to-be naked neighbor, Dick has a very nice body with broad shoulders and toned arms. He's a looker.

Erin is as engrossed in the show as I am. She is rarely this quiet while watching 'reality TV.' She's usually busy doing vulgar running commentary, but not tonight. Tonight, we're both quiet. Erin stuffs more popcorn into her mouth, unable to look away from the window.

The stripper's hands travel up and down Dick's torso and abs. When she reaches for his belt, he takes a step back, then another, pulling her with him, never breaking their kiss. When they reach the padded chair the client usually sits in, Dick spins them around and sits her down on the chair instead.

Dick backs up to the pole, and the stripper points to her sound system with a remote. Music must be playing, because shirtless Dick with his broad, toned back starts to sway his hips, running his hands up and down his chest. Erin's jaw drops and she squees.

"Holy fuck! We're getting a male stripper tonight! Must be one of those guys from the 'Whacker Shack' three blocks down. Those dudes are jacked! Show me whatcha got, Dickie-Boy!"

Erin whoops and fist pumps, grabbing an entire handful of popcorn and stuffing it into her mouth. My eyes are riveted to the window across the street.

Best. Neighbors. Ever.

The woman is squirming in her chair, grabbing her breasts through her clothes and squeezing them, obviously excited about this unexpected turn of events too.

Watching Dick move and how the stripper reacts to him sends my imagination to wild and dangerous territory. Mental pictures of me sitting in that chair, while an unnamed, blue-eyed sexy man dances for my pleasure, has the spot between my legs aching, my chest hurting and my fists clenching. Lust, heartache, and frustration dance a fierce tango inside my body.

"I shouldn't be watching this."

Erin pats my back without looking away from the window.

"Yeah, me neither." Her eyes are still glued to the glass.

I squirm in my seat and try to look away, but a second later my gaze is locked on the guy again.

Dick grabs hold of the pole with one arm and grinds against it suggestively before he squats slowly—languidly—trailing a hand along the pole, like a soft caress. He moves effortlessly. His hips sway slowly, suggesting what's to come. The movement makes me think of another pair of hips that move just as seductively. A naughty part of the back of my mind wants him to do a full frontal, to satisfy the perverse fantasy in my head, but that would only add to my state of permanent sexual frustration.

Dick slowly, in a very leisurely style rises from his squat, and runs a hand through his hair, flexing his arm muscles. He takes a step forward, closer to the woman and points to her. He's saying something to her. She runs one of her hands down her stomach and slides it down into her pants, making me hotter down below and my breathing faster.

Look away, Gina. Look away! Sirens are going off in my head, but my eyes are glued in place, unable to blink.

Her hand moves up and down, her hips rocking slowly at first. The man keeps on moving his hips, watching her, and reaching for his pants. Holy mother of all things porn! He's going to take it all off.

From our vantage point, he seems to be unfastening his jeans but they stay up. With his back to us, it's hard to tell what he is doing. It seems like he's just dancing for the woman while watching her touch herself. The woman is rubbing herself off madly as her hips buck into her hand faster and harder while Dick continues his sexy gyrating.

The woman reaches her climax, made apparent by how her free hand grabs the armrest of the chair, and how her face contorts in obvious pleasure. Her head then sags limply on the back of the recliner, she's completely sated and I envy her even more.

Dick walks to her and gently lifts her up to her feet. They turn so that the stripper's back is now to us. She pushes on Dick's shoulders so that it's his turn to sit. Erin and I are both craning our necks from side to side as if it'll help us see around the stripper and get a better glimpse of Dick's face.

Of course, it doesn't work. It's not until the stripper walks toward her sound system that we get a full view of the gorgeous man sitting in the chair. His chest is all firm muscle, his dark hair a mess, and there's three-day old stubble on his face. His piercing blue eyes are looking into our loft, straight at me, straight into me.

It's Pete.

WALKING THE BAT
September 11th, 7:59pm

"Holy fuck, Gina! Is that...?"

Erin doesn't finish her question or maybe she does but I can't hear her, the pounding in my ears is too loud.

I jump up from the couch and let the bowl of popcorn fall to the floor. In the background, a faint hum carries in tandem with the thrumming in my ears. Erin is saying things, probably very colorful expletives, complaining as she picks up popcorn from off of the floor--again--but that's the least of my worries.

I'm in a daze of anger and envy. I walk slowly toward the window. No, it's not a daze. I'm in shock.

The stripper has started her dance, spinning about the pole, but Pete's eyes remain on me instead of her. His hands are gripping the armrests of the recliner and my nails are digging into my palms. The pain doesn't register.

When I get to the window, unclench my fists and place a hand on the cool glass. Too many emotions are whirling around inside of me to make any sense of them all. I look down to the street and see his bike parked just outside of her building. Strangely enough, my chauffeur, slash bodyguard, slash spy isn't there.

I glance back up.

Pete's still watching me.

The stripper is on her hands and knees, crawling toward him. I want to scream for her to stop.

She can't do this.

Not with him.

Soon, she'll be undressing him.

Soon, she'll be pleasuring him.

She'll be taking him in her mouth before climbing on his lap, and then she'll be fucking the man I'm supposed to marry right before my eyes.

His gaze leaves mine to look at her, and he smiles crookedly. I don't even want to imagine what's about to happen, let alone see it. I've seen him before with another woman, but that was different. I didn't know him then, and he didn't know me. It wasn't even deliberate.

This display isn't about his insatiable need for sex with random women. This show is for my eyes only. This show is purposeful. My jaw locks and my gaze narrows. I'm so angry that my jaw is going to crack.

I turn on my heels and rush toward the door, my hair whipping in my face as I do so.

"Hey! A little help here, Gina?" Erin stops and rests on her heels. She's still on the floor. "Gee? Gina! What the hell? Wait! Where are you going? Don't you want to see how the show ends? Gina!" Erin's face pops up over the backrest of the couch, but I can't look at her.

"I need some air. Laugh at me all you want, Erin, call me whatever names you want, but I can't watch this. I'm going for a walk. Text me when they're done."

Erin stands up and places the bowl on the coffee table. "It's dark out there and way too late to go walking on your own. You'll get mug-rape-killed!"

I put on Pete's old leather jacket and tuck my keys and cell phone securely in the pockets. After opening the door, I grab the baseball bat that Erin keeps there.

"Then I'll take your bat for a walk." I slam the door behind me before Erin can stop me and bolt.

I fly down the stairs. I can't even feel the steps under my feet as they land. Seconds later, I'm outside, taking in a huge gulp of the crisp night air. I start to walk down the street at a fast clip, with a baseball bat resting on my shoulder.

I don't know where I'm going. I just walk, stepping over trash that's been dragged to the curb for pick up.

Pete did this on purpose.

I know he sleeps around, I just don't want to see it. The fact that he deliberately chose her apartment, knowing I'd be watching, just sends his message to me loud and clear.

'I'm a player and I fuck—always have, always will.' I just don't understand why he did it. He's supposed to be my friend.

We're supposed to look out for each other, and not rip each other apart.

I wrap my arms around my middle tighter, trying to stay warm. The bat is still firmly clutched in my hand and I squeeze it until my fingers hurt. FML. How did I get in this spot?

Option one is Pete, my future fiancé and untouchable erotic dream come true, but also my worst nightmare, going against every single value I hold dear.

Option two is Philip, the fairytale, everything I've ever wanted in man just a few months too late.

Maybe it's time I take inventory of my values and do a little reassessing. Maybe I'm the one who has it all wrong. Would it be so bad to have a lover on the side, knowing that Pete and I won't ever have a real marriage? Can I go on living an entire life without the prospect of ever being loved?

My questions go unanswered, and the loud, aggressive rumble of a motorcycle passing on the street jostles me from my thoughts. The sound is thunderous, especially when the bike comes to a stop right ahead of me and the rider gives the engine an extra revving. I look down at my feet and keep on walking, doing my best to ignore Pete. He's probably only here to bring me back home since my leash is nowhere to be found. I'm the Ferro pet running stray through the streets. I manage to pass by him, but not for very long.

Pete puts his hand on my shoulder, stopping me.

"Gina!" Pete's angry voice is muffled from inside his helmet, but it's no less menacing.

"Get away from me, Pete!" I don't bother to turn around. I don't want to see his face.

"Gina, get on the bike."

I feel my self-control slipping away from me, bit by bit. I close my eyes and try to stay calm, but my hands start to shake, so I grip the bat tighter. I try to talk calmly, but my teeth won't unclench, my jaw is locked in anger.

"Get away from me, Pete, I mean it."

"Sulking around the streets alone is dangerous. Stop acting childish and get on the bike. I'm taking you back to your place now."

I spin around to face him.

"Childish? Do you want to see childish? Here! This is childish!"

I lunge toward his precious bike and do what comes naturally. Holding the bat firmly, I take a swing. It comes crashing down on the headlight. Little plastic fragments go flying everywhere. A car drives by and slows down, but doesn't stop. I take another swing, letting out a scream.

"I HATE YOU!"

And I do hate him, just as much as I care for him, too—and I hate myself for it. I put all my emotions into the swing. The bat hits the metal frame. On contact, a resounding gong echoes down the adjacent alley. The bat sends painful vibrations up my arms.

"Have you gone fucking insane?" Pete screams from behind me and circles me with his arms, preventing me from taking another swing at his bike. My chest is heaving and my whole body is trembling with rage.

I stare back at the bike and the bat in my hands, horrified. Oh, my God! What did I just do? I release it as if it were poison. The sound of the metal bat falling to the ground resonates as I watch it bounce from the tip to the handle a couple of times before it comes to rest in the gutter.

Pete has this effect on me and I hate him for it. I hate him for all of it—the erotic passion, the violent jealousy, the attraction that won't disappear no matter how much I wish it weren't there.

This isn't me. I'm not this lunatic. It scares me that Pete can push my buttons so easily. I don't want to be this person.

Pete keeps a tight hold on me for a while. My rage simmers down. My voice is calm, but the words are still filled with raw emotion.

"I hate you, so much. You lying piece of shit."

Pete lets go of me. My feelings are so out of whack that I immediately start to miss his arms holding me tight. His answering voice is stern but lacks conviction.

"Good. You should hate me."

I turn to face Pete. With his helmet on, I can only see the top part of his face, but his eyes show everything. Hurt and sadness. I point toward the general direction of my apartment building and try to talk past the dry lump in my throat.

My body is still so tense that I'm shaking. I want to scream at him, but I keep my rage in check enough to speak.

"Why? Why would you do that? I thought we had a truce?"

Pete unfastens his helmet and takes it off. He has little imprints on his cheeks from where the protective padding was pressing into his cheeks. He runs a hand through his messy helmet hair and lets out a sigh.

"The truce wasn't working for me. This is who I am, Gina, and despite what anyone says or thinks, you can't change that. What do you expect?" He places a palm flat on his chest and smiles as if he's proud. "I'm my father's son. We don't get to choose who we are. We're born into this world and we inevitably become who we are destined to be. This is me. Whether you like it or not, you'll have to get used to the women."

I step toward him, eerily in control now, and shove a finger into his chest.

"You may be your father's son, but I am most definitely not your mother. I am not made of ice and if you deliberately provoke me, you should expect retaliation. This," I say, motioning to the broken bike and discarded bat, "is not how I will spend the rest of my life." I shove his chest, unable to find another outlet for my frustration.

Pete doesn't move. Instead, he lets out another huff of air, but this time it sounds more like a laugh than a sigh.

"You really are a rose, aren't you? Beautiful at first look, but riddled with thorns." His eyes crinkle a bit and his mouth quirks up into a small grin.

"And you're a fucktard, so I guess we're even-steven."

Pete laughs louder, wrapping his arms around me and holding me close to him. I swat at him and try to pull out of his embrace.

"No! You can't have me and have her too. You can't touch me like you care, and then do shit like this!"

"Gina, what do you expect me to do?" His tone is clipped and those blue eyes are wild.

"Anyone and everyone, just not in front of me! I don't want to see you pleasuring other women. I don't want to see you crawl between some chicks legs!"

"Why? Who cares?"

I shove him again, and he takes a pity step back. "I care! Me! I do!"

He takes my shoulders and looks down into my face. "Why?"

"I don't know! I just do. Let go of me." I try to shake out of his grip, but he only holds me tighter. I stiffen against his chest. "You can't do crap like this. I can't take it. I can't."

"Okay, okay. Calm down. It was just a joke." His words sound sincere, but I can't see his face.

I suck in air and keep struggling, trying to pull away, but Pete puts a hand on the back of my head.

"I can't live like this, Peter. I have a heart, and I can't hide it. Even if we aren't together, I don't want to see you having sex with someone else."

His voice is a whisper. "Tell me why, Gina, please."

My stomach flips at the gentle way he says my name. I scold myself for feeling so attached to him and make something up. I know why, but there's no way in hell I'm telling him. He'll rip my heart out of my chest if he knows.

"Because I don't want to see my friends having sex. Ever."

"So, that's a hard, fast rule?"

I nod, and he holds me firmly. I start to relax in his embrace. A smile plays at the edges of my mouth.

Pete rests his head on top of mine and takes a deep breath.

"What the hell am I supposed to do with you?"

"Well, according to page three, paragraph two, article five of your mother's contract, I believe you're supposed to marry me." It was meant as a joke, but it comes out sounding like something more profound, deeper, like a proposal.

I look up and it's a huge mistake. His face is so close to mine now. His smile is gone, and his eyes fill with sorrow. There is so much depth and emotion locked up behind those eyes and I want to help him unleash it. That irrational sliver of hope keeps poking through, making me think that maybe, with time, he'll come around and let himself feel something other than rage and lust.

I can see it. It's right there below the surface.

He looks like he's debating if he should kiss me or not, looking down at my lips and then into my eyes. I'm starting to know that look all too well and, as tempting as it may be, it's my signal to push away.

My phone vibrates, shattering the moment like a mirror smashing to the ground. Pete and I let go of each other and I take a step back. The phone vibrates again and I take it out of my pocket to see who it is. The name Phillip Gambino flashes across the screen. I look up toward Pete, who's now staring at the phone.

"Aren't you going to answer?" he asks softly.

I shake my head, unsure of what I want to do. The phone vibrates a third time. One more and it will go to voicemail.

Pete makes the decision for me when he swipes the screen with his finger, answering the call for me and backing away. I hear Phillip's voice on the other end of the line calling my name, and I put the phone to my ear.

"Hey, Phillip. Yeah, I'm here... No, this isn't a bad time." I look at Pete, wishing he hadn't answered. There's more to say, but it's clear it won't be said now. I clear my throat and take a step away from Pete.

"I was about to call it a night. There's only so much studying I can do... A drink?" My attention is half on the conversation, half on Pete. He's crouched in front of his bike, his boots crunching the plastic shards on the ground. He's assessing the damage, shaking his head.

When I mention going to have a drink, he looks up at me with a sad smile and nods. He mouths, 'Go.'

I tuck a stray strand of hair behind my ear and look away from him. I'm not being chaperoned by the Ferro chauffeur tonight. I'm actually free to spend an evening with Philip without any repercussions. We could stay together all night. I could take out every painful moment of the day on Philip's beautiful body, but...

I glance at Pete and know I want something I can't have. He won't change. Not for me, not for anyone. I plaster a fake smile on my face.

"Sure. That sounds great. Text me the address and I'll meet you there. See you soon." I tuck my phone back in my pocket.

Pete stands up and walks toward me. He jabs a thumb over his shoulder, toward his bike.

"I'd offer you a ride but you see, something happened to my lights. They don't seem to be working for some reason. It might be dangerous." He stuffs his hands in his pockets and looks down at the ground.

"I'm really sorry. I've never done something like that before." I grimace.

His eyes lift slightly, meeting my gaze with mischief.

"I figured as much, but there's no need to lie to me."

My heart races as he steps closer to me. He tips his head to the side and offers an equally crooked grin.

"You enjoyed bashing my bike, and it's okay—I deserved it. I'll just throw this one out and go buy a new one tomorrow."

My face scrunches up. "A new bike? You're just going to leave it in the trash for the garbage guys? What the hell, Ferro?" I'm about to go off on him for being a spoiled brat, but he starts laughing.

"No, a new light. What the hell is wrong with you? Do you get a new car every time you get a ding?" He's smiling so hard that I can see a dimple on his cheek.

I smile coyly and look at my shoe.

"You think I'm soft, don't you?"

His smile widens. I expect him to tease me, to say something that makes me laugh. He looks at my hair and lifts the lock that keeps falling in my eyes.

Pushing it back, he says, "Not at all. Not even a little. I think you're stronger and more alive than anyone I've ever met—you just don't know it yet." His azure gaze locks with mine, searching for something I'm sure is absent.

I smile. "That's a nice thought, but it belongs on a greeting card."

He shakes his head and looks down at his helmet. His voice deepens. "You're finding yourself, and that's fine. You're figuring out what your limits are and how far you're willing to go to get what you want."

"So are you." Pete laughs like it's not true. "You don't see it either, but you will."

He smirks and touches my arms lightly. "If the moment passes me by, be sure to take a picture. I have a really good relationship with a lot of city photographers."

I look at his hand on my arm and then back up into his face. He lets his fingers slip away. I pretend it did nothing. This is going to be my life—a series of lies and smiles—until I'm utterly devoid of any feeling whatsoever.

"I better get going." Pete nods. I hold up my phone. "I'm going to call a cab. You want me to get one for you too?"

"What do you mean?" He looks at me like I've grown an extra head. "I'm going back home on this baby."

Of course, he is. I give Pete a bit of a concerned scowl, but he turns his back to me and walks toward his bike. There's no use in trying to convince him otherwise. He's reckless and couldn't care less what happens to him. Maybe that's why he fights so much.

He swings his leg over, straddles the bike and makes the engine roar to life. I never used to like motorcycles. They represent hoodlums and delinquency. Now, the sound reminds me of Pete. A hoodlum and delinquent, but a friend who somehow needs me.

"Pete!" I call out to him before he puts his helmet back on. He turns around and looks at me, his blue eyes look tired instead of alive and full of life.

"You're not your father, you know. You're you. You don't have to try so hard to be like him if you don't want to."

Pete looks at the cloudless sky. He closes his eyes for a moment and when he looks back down at me, his gaze cuts through me like a carving knife. It's the cocky, arrogant, Pete-the-player look. The hunter, hungry for his next prey. The man who sat in the stripper's chair, waiting to be devoured.

"Yes, I do."

COMING SOON:

LIFE BEFORE DAMAGED
Volume 8
THE FERRO FAMILY

*****

To ensure you don't miss H.M. Ward's next book,
text AWESOMEBOOKS (one word) to 22828
and you will get an email reminder on release day.
*****

Want to talk to other fans?
Go to Facebook and join the discussion!

COVER REVEAL:

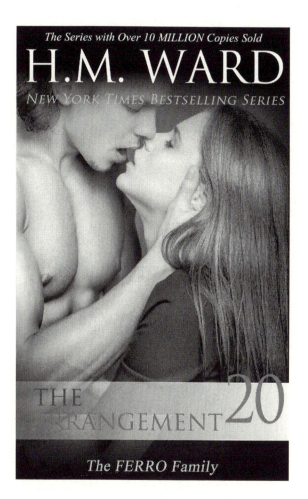

The Series with Over 10 MILLION Copies Sold

H.M. WARD

NEW YORK TIMES BESTSELLING SERIES

THE ARRANGEMENT 20

The FERRO Family

MORE FERRO FAMILY BOOKS

NICK FERRO
~THE WEDDING CONTRACT~
*****

BRYAN FERRO
~THE PROPOSITION~
*****

SEAN FERRO
~THE ARRANGEMENT~
******

PETER FERRO GRANZ
~DAMAGED~
******

JONATHAN FERRO
~STRIPPED~
******

MORE ROMANCE BY H.M. WARD

SCANDALOUS

SCANDALOUS 2

SECRETS

THE SECRET LIFE OF TRYSTAN SCOTT

DEMON KISSED

CHRISTMAS KISSES

SECOND CHANCES

And more.

To see a full book list, please visit:
www.sexyawesomebooks.com/#!/BOOKS

CAN'T WAIT FOR H.M. WARD'S NEXT STEAMY BOOK?

⋆⋆⋆⋆⋆

Let her know by leaving stars and telling her what you liked about
LIFE BEFORE DAMAGED, VOL. 7
in a review!

COVER REVEAL:

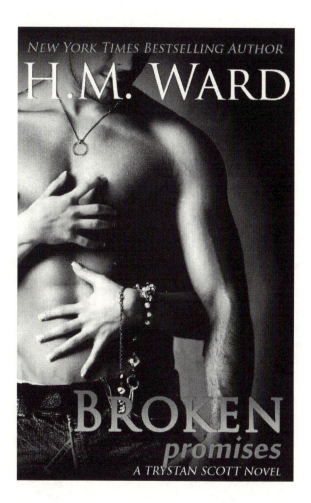

NEW YORK TIMES BESTSELLING AUTHOR

H.M. WARD

BROKEN
promises
A TRYSTAN SCOTT NOVEL

29107680R00078

Made in the USA
San Bernardino, CA
14 January 2016